FREE LANCE
and the
LAKE OF
SKULLS

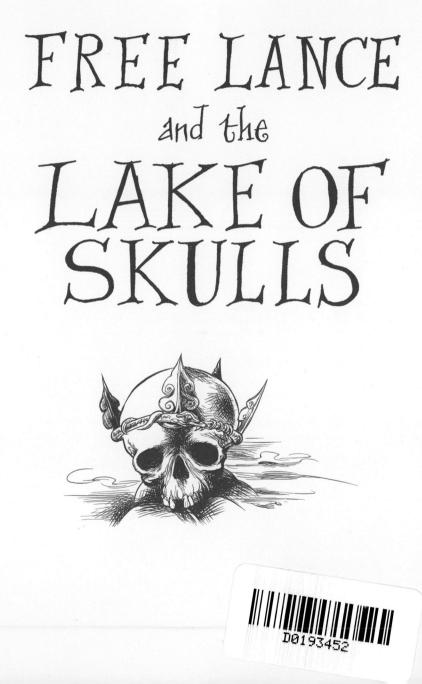

Published in 2017 in Great Britain by
Barrington Stoke Ltd
18 Walker Street, Edinburgh, EH3 7LP

www.barringtonstoke.co.uk

First published by Hodder & Stoughton Ltd, 2003

A CIP catalogue record for this book is available
from the British Library upon request

ISBN: 978-1-78112-714-8

Printed in China by Leo

This book has dyslexia-friendly features

FREE LANCE

and the

LAKE OF SKULLS

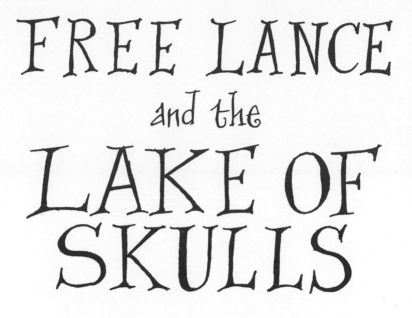

PAUL STEWART

CHRIS RIDDELL

Barrington Stoke

1

"Oy, you!"

I looked up. I was in this flyblown, two-bit tavern, drinking watered-down ale. All of a sudden a heavy great tankard came whistling towards me. I ducked.

Ale slopped all down my front. I cursed under my breath and looked round to see the tankard slam into the face of the little, timid-looking drinker next to me. It struck his jaw with a sound like a hammer splintering wood.

With a low groan he slumped to the floor at my feet. His drink joined the ale down my front. It was spiced mead, if the sickly smell was anything to go by. I was a mess. But not as much of a mess as the little fellow.

Two teeth lay on the floor in front of him. A trickle of blood oozed out over the sawdust.

Behind me, a loud, beast-like roar went up. I turned to see a great hulk of a man lumbering from leg to leg in a slow battle-jig. He was all hairy jowls and heaving gut and I recognised him at once.

His fists were clenched. His bloodshot eyes were wild.

"Come on, if you think you're hard enough!" he bellowed.

'Here we go again!' I thought. 'Why do I always seem to end up in this type of place? You'd think I'd have learned by now. All I wanted was a quiet drink. Is that too much to ask? Is it?'

Given the day I'd had so far, maybe it was ...

*

I'd woken that morning, bitten to blazes. The night before, Jed and I had taken shelter from a storm in a shabby stable. In the early morning light I saw that the whole place was jumping.

Of course, *Jed* was all right. The fleas hadn't touched him. They were too busy gorging on yours truly. As I scratched at the bites, Jed neighed. I could have sworn he was laughing.

I packed up, saddled up and crept out of there, as quiet as a princess breaking wind. I was far out in the back of beyond, where it didn't pay to draw attention to yourself.

Normally, I stick to the castle tournaments, but after the season I'd just had I was prepared to do anything. Exhibition matches, sword displays, even a joust on a village green. I wasn't proud.

I'd knocked over my fair share of big-time knights at the beginning of the year, but then a churned-up field and a second-rate lance had spelled disaster. The lance shattered in my hand and I went down. I was laid up for a month – and my shoulder still hurt when it was cold ...

I'd ended up in the Badlands. Out here every group of run-down hovels boasted a robber baron, and the contests were – how shall I say? – less refined.

It was another beautiful Badlands day. Murky, grey, and so cold it felt like someone jabbing needles into your skin. The sky was the colour of stale gruel, and by late morning an icy drizzle had begun to fall. I felt the old twinge in my shoulder.

I'd heard talk of a contest in a village up ahead, near a mountain lake, and I fancied Jed and my chances against some yokel on a donkey.

Sure enough, I found it on the other side of a scrubby thorn wood. The village was a miserable collection of ramshackle dwellings clustered round one of those low, mud-brick halls that pass for manor houses in these parts. Jed and I went down the muddy main street. There wasn't a villager to be seen.

Jed whinnied and reared up, and his nostrils quivered. I steadied him and told him it was all right – but he had a point. The place stank. The kind of smell that clings to you like a landlady on pay day. But then, that's village life for you – nothing but cabbage water and open sewers. Give me a life on the road any day.

I soon solved the mystery of the missing villagers. They were all standing outside the ropes they'd used to set up a sort of tournament ring, on a muddy patch of grass on the far side of the manor house.

My heart sank. The tournament was nothing more than a wooden club-and-shield contest, winner takes all. Two hefty oafs were in the middle of the ring, battering each other for all they were worth. Blood and sweat spattered the cheering onlookers. A sour-faced chap with a big nose, shifty eyes and heavy, fur-lined robes sat above them on a raised platform. No doubt the lord of the run-down manor, and everything else around.

I'd seen his type a hundred times before. Little men with big ideas who arrived in a place one day with a purse of gold and a gang of thugs. A promise here and a threat there, and pretty soon they were running the place

and putting on all sorts of airs and graces. There's nothing like hosting a tournament to make a man feel like a real lord.

Lord Big Nose caught my eye. "Well, well, well. Look what we have here," he called across. His voice was thin and wheedling. "If it isn't a real-life knight come to take part in our humble contest. How about hand-to-hand combat on foot, sir knight?"

"Jousting's more my area," I shouted back.

Just then, one of the competitors took a blow to the throat and a chop to the back of the neck. He thudded to the ground like a sack of turnips, out for the count, and was dragged away by the heels. The winner raised his club with a toothless grin as the crowd cheered. I turned away.

"You must have travelled far," the wheedling voice said. "Are you sure you wouldn't like to take part?"

I looked back to see a fresh contender climbing into the ring. He was big, hairy and ugly, a great hulk with a face that wouldn't have looked out of place on a vegetable stall – shapeless as a potato and with two great cauliflower ears. His eyes narrowed. "Oy, pretty boy," he grunted. "Fancy your chances?"

I shook my head. Sword play was one thing – I could have filleted Potato Head here like a fat fish fresh from the moat with a few sweeps of my sword. I might have been desperate for money – but not *that* desperate. Fighting with clubs is for mugs.

I climbed back into the saddle and the crowd roared with approval as some poor sap was pushed into the ring. I didn't hang around to watch the fight. I already knew how it would end.

I paused only to hammer a loose nail back into one of Jed's rear hoofs before I left the village. I hoped the horseshoe would hold till I could get him to a blacksmith.

That's the thing about being a free lance – no lord to pay your upkeep. Mind you, I'd tried that once. It hadn't worked out.

That said, it's a good life if you like clean sheets, regular meals, the best armour money can buy – and a fat, pompous lord ordering you around morning, noon and night.

Of course, it
doesn't help when his
lady falls in love with
you! Things had got
pretty complicated
for me on that front.

I ended up breaking the lady's heart, and the lord's nose – and I had to swim the castle moat at midnight to avoid a permanent stay in the dungeons.

No, the bonded life was not for me. I could have made it big, but I wasn't prepared to become some lord's pet knight again. I would just have to hope that Jed didn't end up lame.

By now, the drizzle had turned to a cold, driving rain that numbed my fingers, dulled my mind and played havoc with my shoulder. What was more, I was hungry. My stomach was grumbling like a courtier with corns, and Jed was complaining even louder. The nail in

his shoe had come loose. He was beginning to limp. There was no choice, I had to go back.

"It's all right, boy," I said. "We'll go back and take care of that shoe, then we'll find a place for the night. Fresh straw for you, clean sheets for me. And to hell with the expense."

Jed didn't need me to say it twice. Without so much as a twitch on the reins, he turned and trotted back towards the village.

It was getting dark by the time we hit town for the second time. The grinning blacksmith robbed me blind, but Jed was happy to be in a warm stall for the night. For myself, I'd noticed a warm glow and the sound of laughter coming from a tavern by the green. I left the blacksmith's and headed for it.

Inside, the place was buzzing. I recognised one or two characters from the tournament ring. One was a hefty man with a black moustache and a swollen, bloody nose. The other was a short, pudgy individual with a dirty bandage round his head. I'd seen him getting pummelled in the ring ...

All of a sudden a tall woman was standing in front of me. She had hair the colour of spun gold and a smile that was brighter than a summer morning. She looked me up and down – and it was clear she liked what she saw.

"The name's Nell," she said, and she flashed me that dazzling smile. "I run this place."

"Pleased to meet you, Nell," I said, with my own smile back.

She went a little pink. "Likewise, sir knight, I'm sure," she said. "What can I get you?"

I told her I was looking for a good meal and a warm bed for the night. She could offer both – at a price that made Jed's stall seem like a bargain. 'That's the trouble with being a knight,' I thought, as Nell disappeared into the kitchen. 'You look wealthier than you are and everyone robs you blind. Maybe I should be flattered.'

While I was waiting for my meal I stepped up to the bar and ordered a large ale. I licked my lips as the barman poured the foaming brown nectar from barrel to tankard.

"Thirsty work, knighting and all," someone said.

I nodded. The barman pushed the tankard across the bar. I seized it, raised it to my lips and was just about to drink when a rough voice cut through the friendly babble.

"Oy, you!"

*

So there I was, in this flyblown, two-bit tavern,
ale down my front. The timid-looking drinker
lay at my feet with his jaw stoved in by a
tankard, and a great potato-headed oaf was
lumbering towards me.

"It's you, isn't it?" Potato Head bellowed.
His face came so close to mine I was struck
by his stinking breath. "Isn't it?" he repeated.
"You're that fancy, pretty-boy knight."

2

I met his gaze and kept my voice calm and slow. "I am a knight," I said. "Unbonded. A free lance ..."

The tavern fell still. Potato Head turned to his cronies. "An unbonded knight, if you please," he mocked. "A free *lance*. Very posh." An edge came into his voice. "Unbonded vagabond, more like! A free *loader*!"

An angry rumble went round. I could tell they thought Potato Head had a point. It was time he and I had a little chat.

I pushed my face into his and tried hard to ignore the cabbage breath. Then I told him exactly what I thought of his manners – and I made sure my comments hit home with a series of heavy punches to the stomach.

As he bent over double, I moved to one side and sent a well-aimed boot at his great backside. He went sprawling, cracking his jaw on the floor where he landed.

The crowd fell silent. Then one of them laughed. Then another. Soon, the whole lot of them were cackling like ferrets in a feather quilt.

Potato Head rolled over, rubbed his jaw and climbed to his feet. He spotted the little fellow still knocked out on the floor and gave him a vicious kick in the ribs.

The crowd booed.

"Yeah?" Potato Head sneered as he looked round. "What are you going to do about it, eh?"

The crowd fell still once more. I stepped forwards. "How about this?"

I punched him. A swift jab to his jaw. He didn't know what had hit him. I punched him again – a punishing left hook to the head.

His neck jerked backwards. His eyes dimmed. But he didn't fall over.

I'd seen this before. The great hulk was too stupid to know when to drop.

The crowd remained silent as I raised a single finger and prodded him in the chest.

Potato Head grunted, twisted and fell to the floor with a loud thud and a flurry of sawdust.

The crowd went wild.

Just then, the kitchen door flew open and Nell burst in and demanded to know what was going on. The crowd nodded towards yours truly. They were a fickle bunch.

Nell strode round to the front of the bar.

She looked at the timid drinker who was just coming round. She looked at Potato Head out cold. She put two and two together and came up with five.

"I'll have no trouble-makers in my inn," she told me, and her green eyes flashed with anger. "Get out!"

I didn't argue. By the way she was fussing over Potato Head – opening his tunic and patting his head – it was clear whose side she was on. He was a local. I was a stranger. End of story.

I turned to go. At that moment, a thin, wheedling voice broke the silence.

"Not so fast."

I turned and looked up into the gallery. There was the big-nosed, sour-faced lord in the fur-lined robes I'd seen at the tournament. He leaned over the balcony.

"We meet again, sir knight." He raised an eyebrow. "You handle yourself well," he said, nodding down at Potato Head. "You've defeated our champion, here."

Out of the corner of my eye, I could see Nell pouting.

"You and I should talk," Lord Big Nose said. "Nell, refill our guest's tankard."

I knew what was about to come. "Not interested," I said, and I turned to go.

Behind me, I heard Lord Big Nose give an unpleasant chuckle. He clicked his fingers.

In an instant, three armed stooges appeared from the shadows, with their crossbows raised and pointed at me. I turned back. A triumphant smile was playing over his Lordship's thin lips.

"Maybe I will have that drink after all," I said.

3

"You could be just the person I'm looking for," his Lordship said, as I tucked into the meal Nell had served up at last.

I nodded as I spooned up my stew, but I said nothing. The pair of us were sitting across from one another at his table in the upper gallery. Below us, the tavern was rowdy. It was as though nothing had happened – and that's the way I liked it. But Lord Big Nose wasn't about to let me forget.

"I liked the way you took care of yourself down there," he told me.

"The bigger they come, the harder they fall," I murmured.

"That was why I organised the contest this afternoon," he went on. "To find someone to carry out a little job for me. Someone tough, fearless – who knows how to take care of himself ..."

It was clear I wasn't going to have a chance to finish my meal in peace. I laid my spoon down.

"Course, I'd make it worth your while," he went on. "And I can see from your armour and weapons that you could do with a piece of gold or two. Not to mention that old nag you rode into town on."

That riled me. Jed might not be as young as he once was, but he was a pure-bred Arbuthnot warhorse. Normally, I would have put old Big Nose right on a few points. But with the crossbows still glinting in the shadows, I knew this was neither the time nor place to discuss horse-breeding. I sat back in my chair and folded my arms.

"So, what's the deal?" I said.

His words buzzed round inside my head like flies in a stable. I'd heard it all before. The promise of easy money. The offer of good lodgings and better feasting. The flattering claim that the task should be simpler than herald duty at a banquet. For a man like me.

A pack of lies, of course, every word of it.

Trouble was, it was the end of the tournament season – and it had been a lousy season at that. Of course, if I was a bound knight, I'd winter up in some castle or other while I perfected my sword play and honed my lancing skills. But I'm a free lance. There'd be no cosy castle for me this winter. I'd be lucky if the little I'd earned this season kept me fed into the new year.

I stared back at the narrow, shifty eyes in front of me. Sickening as it was, Lord Big Nose was looking like my one hope. What was more, I didn't like to admit it, but he was right. The whole thing *did* sound right up my street.

This was the deal.

There was an island.

Craggy, misty, stuck in the middle of a lake in the mountains. The Lake of Skulls. That was where he wanted me to go.

There, I'd find a huge pile of skulls. (The clue was in the name.) My job was to climb up to the very top, where I'd find the skull of an ancient king still wearing his gold crown. I had to take the crown and return it to Lord Big Nose, at which point he'd cough up a purse full of gold crowns, and free ale and board for the whole winter.

I could tell by the greedy way he licked his lips when he spoke of the crown that it meant a lot to him. Who knows why he didn't just go and get it himself. Probably he believed the place was cursed or something. They believe in that stuff, these Badlands yokels.

Anyway, I wasn't asking questions. Lord Big Nose might well be a snivelling little man with more money than sense, but he needed my services and I needed his money. That – I'm sorry to say – is the way of the world these days. Besides, how difficult could the job be?

I was about to find out ...

4

I finished off my meal and mopped up the greasy remains of the stew with a hunk of bread. Lord Big Nose was still going on about the crown. It wasn't worth very much at all, he said, but it had sentimental value. It was clear he didn't want me to know how much it meant to him.

I smiled and nodded in what I hoped were all the right places. To be honest, I wasn't really listening. I was thinking about Jed.

I wouldn't be able to take him with me. I didn't fancy leaving him tethered up by the edge of the lake, and taking him over to the island wasn't an option. I didn't want to risk losing my most valuable possession in a night swim in some icy mountain lake – and rowing boats and horses are not a good combination. I knew I had no other choice but to stable him up in the village until my return.

"So it's settled then," his Lordship said. He climbed to his feet and smiled that simpering smile of his. "Let's shake on it."

I gripped his hand. It was like shaking hands with a dead fish.

"Bring the crown to my manor," he told me, "and I'll have your money waiting for you. Good luck, sir knight – I trust you'll leave at once."

With that, he turned and left, with his bodyguards and armed henchmen clumping down the stairs after him like trolls.

I snorted. If Big Nose thought I was about to set off on his little quest in the middle of the night, he had another thought coming.

I'd booked a bed for the night, and I was going to get good use out of it. I scraped the chair back and headed upstairs.

My room was small and dingy, and I banged my head on a low beam.

But the bed had clean linen on it, and the mattress was soft. *Very* soft …

*

I woke up to the sound of barrels clanking below my window. The sun was already up. I cursed myself for over-sleeping, as I jumped up, splashed water over my face and headed downstairs. Nell was in the bar with a mop in her hands and a bucket at her feet. She flashed me one of her dazzling smiles. There were obviously no bad feelings.

"Sleep well?" she said with a bright smile.

I told her I had. Despite, or maybe because of the blow to my head, I'd slept like a log. Now it was time to set off. I turned down her offer of breakfast, settled up and headed for the blacksmith's.

Jed was happy to see me. He nuzzled against me as I untied him, and blew billowy clouds of warm air on my hands. He hated it when we were

separated, and I felt a twinge of guilt that I was going to leave him behind all over again. Still, I had no other option.

The blacksmith sent me to some stables on the outskirts of the village. They were run-down, shabby buildings, but the half-dozen horses in the battered stalls looked well-groomed and content. Jed was less sure.

As I slipped down from the saddle, he reared up and pounded the air with his front hoofs.

"Frisky, ain't he?" a voice said.

I turned to see a thin, weasel-faced man, with darting eyes and twitchy side-whiskers. He reached up and pulled down on Jed's reins with remarkable strength for one so small. Then he leaned forwards and whispered, first in one ear, then the other. Jed quivered and fell still.

"Impressive," I told him.

"I've always had a way with horses," he said. "Like my father, and his father before him."

I knew I'd come to the right place. Jed would be fine while I was away. I handed over three groats as a down-payment.

"So, where are you heading?" Weasel Face asked as the coins jangled in his pocket.

"Just up into the mountains," I said. "Not horse country."

He drew his breath
in through his teeth.
"Don't tell me," he said,
"the Lake of Skulls, I'll be
bound. To retrieve that
accursed crown."

He shuddered. I listened.

"We locals know when to leave well alone," he told me. "It doesn't do to go stirring things up at the lake. It's an ancient place, full of ancient things – and it should be respected, if you ask me. But it's no good telling his Lordship that. Oh, no. He just wants that crown and he doesn't care how he gets it – or what trouble he causes. Course, he's too lily-livered to go up there himself, isn't he? So he sends others to do his dirty work for him." He fixed me with his eyes. "You're not the first and you won't be the last. His Lordship won't rest till he's got his hands on it."

"What happened to the others?" I asked. I tried to keep my voice light. I didn't like the way Weasel Face was shaking his head.

"I wouldn't like to say," he said, and he pointed at the stalls. "But put it this way, not one of them has ever come back for his horse."

I patted Jed's flank. "Don't worry, Jed, old son," I said. "I'm not planning on being a foot-slogger for any longer than I have to."

I tried to sound relaxed, but I had to admit I was beginning to get a bad feeling in the pit of my stomach. Perhaps it was too much ale. Or perhaps it was the look old Weasel Face had – the look of someone who thought he'd just inherited a pure-bred Arbuthnot charger – and three groats into the bargain.

"Tell me," I said, and I slipped another groat from my pocket. "What exactly *do* you know about the Lake of Skulls?"

*

I knew from Lord Big Nose that the lake lay on the far side of the vast pine forest to the north-east of the village. He'd failed to mention how close the trees were packed together or the dense vines underneath. With my sword drawn, I hacked my way through. But it was slow going. Just as well I'd left Jed behind.

As I battled on, I mulled over Weasel Face's far-fetched tale. It was the tale of an ancient king who fell in love with an enchantress and

made her his queen. The poor sap discovered his beloved and her handmaids dabbling in the dark arts. He had *them* banished, and *her* executed – but not before he'd forced her to make him an enchanted crown. It was meant to make him top-dog around these parts.

But something went wrong. Who knows what? According to the legend, the king's head now sits on a pile of skulls in the centre of the island. He still wears the enchanted crown – a band of gold in the shape of a coiled serpent, with the words of the queen's spell engraved around it.

'Nice touch,' I thought. I smiled to myself as I remembered old Weasel Face say it with his eyes closed in respect.

"He who wears the serpent's band,
Shall be dreaded across the land,
Destined to be raised up on high,
And worshipped till the lake runs dry."

I chuckled. No wonder the story had got
Lord Big Nose all excited. It was amazing
what some people chose to believe. Mind you,
so long as there was the promise of a purse
full of gold, I wasn't complaining.

It was dark inside
the forest and, by the
time I reached the other end,
I found it was dark *outside* as
well. The sun had set and the fat
yellow moon was just dragging itself
up over the horizon. It shone across the
rippled water of the vast mountain lake before
me. As I peered ahead into a thin mist that
hung over the water, I could just make out the
island in the middle.

I marked the place where I'd come out of
the forest with a rock so I could follow my own
path back. Then I set off along the side of the

lake. I soon came to a rickety wooden jetty.
Tied up at the end – just as old Big Nose had
promised it would be – was a small boat made
of animal hides. A coracle.

I stepped in. The small boat rocked from
side to side. I sat down quick smart. The last
thing I wanted was to fall in – if you've ever
attempted front crawl in a breast-plate and
leg armour, you'll know why. I've seen stones
swim better!

The moon was high now and I could see
the island clearly. It didn't look too far
away. I untied the rope, picked up
the paddle and pushed off from the jetty.

I've never liked coracles. I
mean, don't get me wrong. They're
fine for fat monks who want to do a spot
of fishing. But if you actually want to get
anywhere, forget it! A horse bucket would
be faster.

It took ages for me to get into a steady forward rhythm. By that time the wind had got up, thick mist was coiling off the choppy water and the moon kept disappearing behind the clouds. I'm not the type to believe in magic, but believe me, there was something evil about the place. It made my flesh creep.

I thought I'd feel better when I got across the lake.

I thought wrong.

5

The island was a mass of giant black rocks,
slippery and covered with moss. Just landing
the coracle was a challenge in itself. When at
last I managed to scramble ashore onto a cold,
slimy rock, my hands were grazed and my
knees battered black and blue.

The wind had grown stronger, and the
whole place was filled with moans and sighs
as it howled through the gaps between the
boulders. No wonder the island had a bad
name among the Badlands yokels. I might
be a tournament knight from the castle belt,
but when it came to the Lake of Skulls, I was
beginning to see their point.

I started to climb. If I could get to the top of the jumble of huge rocks, I'd be able to take my bearings. That is, if I didn't break my neck first. And all the while, the wind howled, and the mist coiled, and the moonlight came and went ...

At last I reached the top and sank to my knees, panting like a friar's donkey. It was a while before I got my breath back and was in any state to take in my surroundings.

I was on a platform of rock, as flat as an out-of-tune minstrel. Just then, the moon burst out from behind a passing cloud. It shone down on a tall stack of what looked like large white rocks, not a hundred yards in front of me. I headed towards it, hoping the moon would shine long enough for me to get there.

The howling grew louder. The mist coiled round my legs, my chest, my head. It tasted stale, like a gulp of yesterday's ale. The only good thing was that the moon kept shining.

Then, as the stack loomed up in front of me, I wished it hadn't.

The white rocks were glaring at me. Each and every one. They weren't rocks at all. They were skulls. Hundreds of skulls, piled up high, one on top of the other – and at the very top, there it was.

The skull with the gold crown.

It wasn't a nice feeling meeting the black gaze of thousands of skulls, but I could cope with feelings. Perhaps Lord Big Nose was right after all. Perhaps this was a routine job. I wouldn't have minded a bit more of a challenge. But then, after the season I'd had, I reckoned I was due a lucky break.

I started up the pile of skulls. They shifted beneath my feet, so skull knocked against skull with every step.

Half way up, the toe of my boot got stuck in an eye-socket. I stumbled and almost fell back. As I grabbed hold of the skull above me to steady myself, its jawbone came away in my hand. It's a good job I'm not squeamish. But then, as I always say, it's the living that do you harm, not the dead.

Then again, as I climbed higher and higher, the way the colour of the skulls changed was hard to ignore. Brown to yellow to gleaming white. Those at the bottom must have been there for decades, centuries even. Closer to the top, some of them looked a little too fresh for my liking.

One of the skulls had scraps of hair still attached. Another had bits of tattered skin clinging to the bone …

I thought of the horses in Weasel Face's stable. Perhaps I was looking at their owners.

I was near the top of the skull mountain now, and the crown was almost within my grasp at last. I reached for the band of gold. The skulls creaked and cracked beneath my feet as my fingertips grazed the glittering scales of the serpent on the crown.

Just a little bit further!

My grip closed round the crown. I lifted it as gently as I could. The crown came free.

So did the skull.

It slipped from the top and bounced down the pile of skulls, making a sound like a lame horse on cobble-stones. It bounced all the way down to the bottom and landed with an

echoing thud on the rocks below. It lay there
and grinned up at me.

The next instant, an ear-splitting screech
shattered the stillness of the misty night air.
For a moment, I imagined it was the skull. But
only for a moment.

Below me, something was heading my way. Something big, hairy and, by the sound of that screech, pretty angry. As it reached the foot of the skull mountain, it threw back its head and shot me a look of pure, venomous hatred.

I could hardly believe my eyes. It was the biggest, hairiest hag I'd ever seen, with foul, matted hair and snarling fangs. She was big. She was ugly. And she was getting bigger and uglier the closer she got. I grasped the crown and skidded and jumped my way down the far side of the mountain of skulls. Then I set off across the rocks.

The hag screeched with rage. A blood-chilling noise, a cross between a wounded bear and a roaring furnace.

I tucked the crown into my belt and headed for a tall rock to my right. Then I ducked down out of sight behind it and struck off to my left. That was the way I'd climbed

up. With a bit of luck, if I kept my head down, the swirling mist and shifting moonlight would keep me hidden while I clambered back down again. I'd be in that coracle and away before you could say ...

"Hell's teeth!" I yelled, and stopped in my tracks.

The hag must have taken a short cut across the rocks. Now she was standing in front of me, blocking my path.

She grinned at me, and her slavering teeth glinted as she tossed a razor-sharp blade from hand to hand. She nodded towards the crown.

I smiled back. "Nothing personal," I said. The hag's face betrayed no sign of understanding. "I'm just doing a favour for a lord I know. Perhaps you've heard of him – little chap, big nose ..."

Without warning, the hag lunged forwards and her face contorted with rage. I drew my sword as she swung her evil blade. There was a screaming clash of metal as the weapons struck one another. A violent jolt juddered through my entire body. It knocked me off balance and sent me tumbling backwards.

The hag bellowed and slashed at me with her blade as I flapped out of the way like a pike out of water. The blade nicked my shoulder, too close for comfort. I could smell her stinking breath as she closed in for the kill.

I slid round on the greasy surface of the rock and used an old jousting trick I hadn't tried since I was a squire. The Jester's Gambit, a standing backflip with trailing sword arm. It took me straight over the hag's head.

My sword met with resistance. I heard a gasp and a gurgle, and the sound of

the hag's blade clattering down onto the rocks beside me as I landed.

At the same moment, a cloud passed and the moonlight streamed down brighter than ever. I found myself staring at the hag before me. Her eyes glinted, her teeth gleamed. There was blood, pouring down her front, black as pitch. But I knew I had to make sure. The last time I'd failed to finish off a wounded attacker, I'd almost paid the ultimate price. I wasn't about to make the same mistake again.

With a grunt of effort I pulled my sword free and swung it through the air with both hands. The blade whistled. For a moment, the hag remained standing. The next, she collapsed. Her body fell one way, her head, the other.

And I was out of there, faster than a hound on a boar-hunt.

By the time I arrived back at the coracle
I was wet with sweat and panting like a dog.
I'd done it. I'd retrieved the crown, and slain
the creature who'd been guarding it into the

bargain. Now all I needed to do was get it back to Lord Big Nose and claim my fee. I'd never been so pleased to see a coracle in my life.

I climbed down into it. 'The worst,' I thought to myself, 'is over.'

Little did I know that the worst was still to come.

6

As I pushed out into the choppy waters of the lake, the coracle bucked beneath me like a wild jousting pony. Then, as I reached down for the paddle, I saw it.

Huge, it was, gnarled and hairy, with lake water glistening on its knuckles – a monstrous great hand that gripped the side of the boat.

Quick as an eel, I grabbed the paddle and smashed it down on the grasping fingers.

The coracle lurched. The hand let go and slid beneath the water.

I drew my sword and searched the murky depths for the hand's owner. If truth be told, I already had an idea of who that might be ...

There was a sudden splash and I felt a vice-like grip fasten round my leg. Before I

knew it, I was dragged off my feet and into the icy water. I swallowed a lungful before I remembered to close my mouth. I was sinking like a castle cat in a sack of stones. Like I said before, armour and water don't mix.

The next instant, I felt two gigantic hands close round my throat. They held on tight.

My eyes cleared for a moment, and I saw that it was just as I'd feared. My attacker was a second hag. She was older, stronger, and twice as big as the first. There was also a family resemblance, if her ugly mug was anything to go by. It wasn't only her size and power that made her so dangerous, but the fact that she was out for revenge. I had killed her sister. From the look in those bloodshot eyes, I knew that this one was personal.

The water boiled as the pair of us thrashed about. I was desperate to break the hag's lethal grip – and she was just as desperate to hang on.

I twisted and turned, I kicked and punched – but even when my blows struck their target, the hag held on for grim death. She wouldn't be satisfied until she had squeezed the last drop of life out of me.

My lungs were burning, and there was a ringing in my ears. Any moment now, I was going to black out. I knew I had to do something – and fast!

All of a sudden, I let my body go limp. My feet grazed the bottom of the lake and my arms dropped to my side. I closed my eyes.

The hag's grip seemed to tighten, then slowly relax. She rose to the surface with me clamped under one of her huge arms. As we surfaced, the hag gulped down huge lungfuls of air. I snatched tiny, silent breaths and played dead for all I was worth.

As slowly as I could, I closed my hand around the handle of the knife at my belt. The hag waded onto the shore and climbed up onto a boulder, still clutching me tight.

Then she let me go. I dropped, with a thud, onto the cold rock.

And there I lay, like a fish on a serving platter, not moving so much as a muscle. I was good. Very good.

The hag bent down and sniffed at me, and her wet, matted hair brushed my face. She looked me over, up and down, before she settled on my right leg.

She lifted it with one great paw and pulled
off my shin-guard with the other. Then she
rolled back my stocking, and looked at my
bare shin the way a greedy man eyes a leg of
pork.

She licked her lips and bared her yellow
fangs. The stench of her breath was vile. I
sprang up and, with one sharp, punching
thrust, drove the blade of my knife into the
hag's heart.

A look of bewilderment flickered across her face as she staggered backwards. She let out a low gurgling sound, deep in her throat. She coughed. She spluttered. Blood trickled down from the sides of her mouth as she collapsed and rolled off the boulder, back into the water.

The Lake of Skulls fell still.

With the crown hanging from my belt, I went to find the upturned coracle. Thank goodness, it hadn't drifted off. I turned it over, climbed in and started paddling for the second time.

It was only when I got half way across the lake that I stopped to look back. Far behind me was the pile of skulls, still gleaming in the moonlight. I snorted. To think that, as I'd reached up for the crown, I'd wished for a bit more of a challenge. Well, that would teach me!

Just then, the water boiled to my left. It was probably just a carp or a pike. But I wasn't hanging around to find out. I seized the paddle with both hands, then I raced across the lake faster than a jester with his tights on fire.

By the time I reached the jetty I was dripping with sweat. Every muscle in my body was knotted with effort. As I climbed back onto dry land, my legs wobbled beneath me.

To be honest, I'd have liked to rest up for a while. But the greater the distance between me and the Lake of Skulls the better, and just then I was still too close.

I pressed on.

7

It wasn't long before I came to the rock marker that I'd left. I made my way back down the path I'd cut through the forest. It should have been easier going but I was cold, tired and half choked to death, and I made heavy weather of it. To make matters worse, I was soaked to the skin and my armour was beginning to play up.

My feet squelched, and every stitch of clothing on my back was heavy with water. My shin-guards groaned with every step I took. The armour around my arms was on the verge of seizing up completely.

I tried to think of something else – like the warm, soft bed back at the tavern. But it was no good. As I trudged on, the mattress of soft pine-needles beneath my feet began to look more and more inviting.

I told myself to get a grip. One night in a feather bed and I was going soft. Besides, there was something else urging me on. The thought of Lord Big Nose. I couldn't wait to see the look of surprise on his smug, arrogant face when I handed over the crown – and the pain when he handed me my fee.

Day was breaking by the time the trees began to thin out. I found myself back on a narrow track that led into the village. I pushed the crown behind my breast-plate to conceal it, and set off.

My first stop would be the stables, to check on Jed. As I drew close I could hear voices inside. Two voices. One belonged to Weasel Face – nasal, high, squeaky. The other was deeper, lower, gravelly. They were in the middle of some deal or other. I was on my guard.

"Twenty gold sovereigns," Gravel Voice was saying. "If you throw in the Arbuthnot."

"You drive a hard bargain, so you do," Weasel Face whined. "Still, needs must … Twenty gold pieces, it is."

I strode forwards. "Not so fast," I said.

Weasel Face spun round. His face fell. "You," he said. "I didn't think you'd be back."

"Sorry to disappoint you," I said, "but I've come for my horse. Big grey Arbuthnot, goes by the name of Jed – or had you forgotten?"

"The Arbuthnot's yours?" Gravel Voice said. He looked downcast.

"That's right, slime-ball," I said. "And he's not for sale."

I untied Jed and led him from the stall. Then I mounted up, turned back and flicked two groats at old Weasel Face. They landed in the straw at his feet.

"What I owe you," I told him. "Oh, and you can go ahead and sell those other horses," I added. "Their owners won't be back, trust me."

I flicked Jed's reins and we were off.

Weasel Face called out. "Did you find it, then? Did you find the serpent crown?"

I made no reply. That was for me to know and him to wonder. My next stop was Lord Big Nose's run-down manor house. I'd save the story till then.

*

The low sun cast long shadows across the track. The sky was pink. Bad weather was on its way. I passed the green and was about to turn at the tavern, when I heard a voice I knew.

"You're back, brave sir knight! I was afraid I'd seen the last of you." It was Nell the tavern keeper, and her voice was soft and tender.

"I didn't know you cared." I smiled, reining in Jed.

"Oh, sir knight, of course I do." She tossed her golden hair. "You look tired. Come inside and have a drink. I've got a place by the fire, just for you."

"You have?" I said. She'd really got my attention now.

"Of course. And, sir knight," she went on, "I'd be honoured if you'd let me join you." She flashed her big green eyes at me.

"Well, just a quick ale, maybe," I said.

Jed gave an angry neigh and stamped his foot as I tied him up. I followed Nell towards the tavern.

"Not that way," she said as I made for the front door. "Here, this is the door for my special guests."

She took me in a small side entrance. It was dark and warm inside. A fire flickered in a grate and a large chair waited for me by a table with a foaming tankard.

"Help yourself," Nell said, and she closed the door.

I was about to reply, when I was beaten to it by a gruff voice behind me.

"Don't mind if I do," it said.

Before I could look round, I heard a strange rustling sound, followed by a low hiss. I felt my head explode.

Everything went white, then black.

Then, nothing.

8

I was woken by the feel of something warm and wet sliding across my head and down my cheek. For a terrifying moment, I thought I was back on the island, and that one of the hags had come back to finish me off.

My eyes snapped open – to see Jed standing beside me. His neck was lowered and he was licking my face.

"Jed," I murmured as I looked up into his soft, furry face. "What happened?"

Jed whinnied and scraped his hoof on the ground. I pulled myself up, and winced as a

bolt of pain shot across my skull and down my spine. I looked round.

I was back in the stables, sharing a stall with Jed. 'How did I get here?' I asked myself. The pain was now a dull throb at the back of my head.

"Awake, are you?" a familiar voice asked. It was Weasel Face, with a bowl and a cloth in his hand, standing in front of me. "Found you in the gutter outside the tavern," he cackled.

"Blind drunk, so Nell said. Had to throw you out, by all accounts."

"Nell!" I cursed, and my hands flew to my breast-plate. The crown was, of course, gone.

"Still, it was the least I could do after the little mistake with your horse, here," Weasel Face said.

"Yes, yes," I said, as I tried to clear my head. "Don't mention it. How long have I been out?"

"Oh, I found you this morning at sun up, and it's now …" He squinted past me at the patch of sky in the window. "Almost sun down."

I groaned and brushed the straw from my shoulders.

"Look after Jed for me," I told Weasel Face. "I'll be back before morning. And try not to sell him while I'm gone!"

I left, with Weasel Face still cackling at my
little joke.

*

The noise coming from the tavern as I drew
closer was as rowdy and loud as ever. There
was laughter and the babble of conversation,
there was the clinking of tankards and shifting

of chairs, and behind it all, the sound of a fiddle, flute and tabor playing foot-stomping reels.

I stepped up to the door and walked in.

Every eye in the place turned towards me. The laughter and chatter ceased. The band stopped playing. 'Nothing like a friendly welcome,' I thought – and this was *nothing* like a friendly welcome.

I heard a voice from behind me. "Nasty bump, you've got there, stranger."

I turned. It was Nell. She was smiling, but it wasn't a pleasant smile. It was then I noticed the character beside her, with his hefty hand resting on her shoulder. Potato Head. As our eyes met, he grinned. Again, it wasn't pleasant.

"You want to be careful who you pick fights with, pretty boy," he said.

Just then, a second voice called down from the gallery. Lord Big Nose.

"Sir knight," he said, "I'm afraid you are too late."

I looked up. He was leaning against the balustrade, with a smug look on his face and the gold serpent crown on his head. In the

shadows behind him, his henchmen had their crossbows primed.

"As you can see, our champion here has beaten you to it," he said. He looked down at Potato Head, who patted the bulging leather money-pouch tied to his belt. "But thank you so much for all your trouble." Lord Big Nose smirked. "Better luck next time, eh?"

I knew when I was beaten. You had to, in my line of business. Lord Big Nose up there didn't care how he got his creepy serpent crown. And as for old Potato Head, he was just doing what came naturally. No, it was Nell I was disappointed in.

"Nothing personal, you understand," she said.

I nodded. I'm sure she meant it. It was hard to have got so far only to have been caught off-guard in a moment of carelessness. But then that was the risk every free lance had to take.

"No bad feelings, then," she said. "Have a tankard of ale before you leave. On the house."

There was something in her voice that suggested she felt bad about tricking me. I hoped so.

"All right," I said at last. "Make it a large one!"

"Don't push your luck," Nell said, as she picked up a small tankard. Perhaps she didn't feel so bad after all. I shrugged and took my drink to the far corner.

Soon, the chatter struck up again, drinking was resumed, the musicians began playing – and everyone seemed to forget about me altogether. Which was just as well, as I didn't feel much like chatting.

Lord Big Nose was holding court up in the gallery, talking loudly about how he was going to rule the world. No one could resist him now that he wore the serpent crown. And those Badlands yokels cheered his every word.

I had another drink.

Maybe it was the whack on the head, maybe it was the ale, or the heat from the open fire, but pretty soon I nodded off. When I awoke, the roaring log fire had turned to smouldering embers, and there were snoring bodies everywhere. I'd missed one hell of a party.

It was high time I left. I made my way across the room, trying not to step on the bodies on the floor. One of them turned over and mumbled in his sleep, "Pretty-boy knight."

It was Potato Head. He was dead to the world after what looked like a barrel or three of ale. A smile played over his lips. It was clear he was enjoying his dream.

I bent down and untied the leather thong attached to his belt. The heavy purse fell into my hand.

"Pleasant dreams," I murmured as I pocketed the gold. Potato Head gave a contented grunt. I smirked. He'd be smiling on the other side of his face when he woke up.

As I turned to leave, I felt something wet hit my cheek. I looked up at the gallery. Lord Big Nose was slumped over his table. I could see his fur-lined shoulders outlined against the open window.

'He's passed out and spilled his wine,' I thought. 'Just another petty tyrant with big ideas and no head for drink.'

I left and headed back to the stables.

Jed gave a soft whinny when I appeared. He was as pleased as I was to be leaving this godforsaken Badlands hole at last. I untied the rope, climbed into the saddle and took up the reins.

We headed back up the main street, past the tavern and out of town. As we approached the crossroads, a dark shape darted across our path and Jed reared up in fear.

I fought with the reins and at last I managed to calm him down.

It wasn't like Jed to be so spooked – but then I didn't blame him. My own heart was racing, and a cold, clammy sweat clung to me.

"Steady, Jed," I said, as I reined him back. "We can take it easy now."

Jed snickered, and I wiped the sweat from my face. I looked at my hand. It was red with blood – blood that wasn't mine.

I remembered the tavern. Lord Big Nose slumped at the table, the spilt wine dripping from the balcony onto my face. Now I realised, with a jolt, that it wasn't wine ...

"He who wears the serpent's band,
Shall be dreaded across the land,
Destined to be raised up on high,
And worshipped till the lake runs dry."

It all fell into place, and I could see the whole appalling picture.

The headless body of Lord Big Nose slumped by the open window. The third hag returning to the Lake of Skulls to place a fresh head wearing the serpent's gold crown on top of the pile of skulls.

Lord Big Nose would be worshipped all right – and feared and dreaded. But not in quite the way he thought.

I hadn't liked Lord Big Nose, not from the first moment I'd clapped eyes on him. But that didn't stop me feeling a pang of pity for the poor, stupid sap. No one deserved that fate.

Then again, one thing was for sure – the villagers would be a lot better off without him.

I still don't believe in magical crowns and elixirs of eternal life. That kind of stuff's for fairy tales. No, if there's anything that this little escapade has taught me, it's this.

Be careful what you wish for, because you might just get it.

It was a good lesson. I only hoped that I'd be able to stick to it myself. If I kept the thought of Lord Big Nose fresh in my mind, it shouldn't be hard.

Then again, as a free lance, I was dependent on the whims of others and anything was possible. This time I'd survived, and with a pouch of money that should see me through the winter months. Next time, I might not be so lucky.

It was all so uncertain. And yet, in a way, I guess that's exactly what I like about this way of life. The thrill of the chase. The head-rush of battle. The dicing with death. Call me a fool, but despite everything, I'm not about to give up being a free lance.

At least, not just yet.